E

Moss   Moss, Marissa

In America

DUE DATE

IN AMERICA

WRITTEN & ILLUSTRATED BY

Marissa Moss

DUTTON CHILDREN'S BOOKS · NEW YORK

To Walter Mayer, my grandpa;

to Samuel Gardner, Sol Kupperman, Zwecia Srolowitz, and Sarah Cohen;

and to Isadore Louis Stahl, who told me "the prune story." And to all others

who had—and have—the courage to leave their homes and families

for the great unknown, risking all for freedom.

Library of Congress Cataloging-in-Publication Data
Moss, Marissa.   In America/written and illustrated by Marissa Moss.—1st ed.   p.   cm.
Summary: While Walter and his grandfather walk to the post office, Grandfather recounts
how he decided to come to America, while his brother, Herschel, stayed in Lithuania.
ISBN 0-525-45152-8   [1. Grandfathers—Fiction.   2. Emigration and immigration—
Fiction.   3. Jews—United States—Fiction.]   I. Title.   PZ7.M8535In
1994   [E]—dc20   93-26885   CIP   AC

Published in the United States 1994 by Dutton Children's Books,
a division of Penguin Books USA Inc.
375 Hudson Street, New York, New York 10014
Designed by Adrian Leichter
Printed in Hong Kong   First edition
1 3 5 7 9 10 8 6 4 2

W ho are these people, Grandpa?" asked Walter.

"Don't you recognize me?" said Grandpa. "That's me, and that's my brother, Herschel. Your great-uncle. That picture was taken a long time ago and far, far away, where I used to live before I came to America."

"Where was that?" Walter asked.

"A small village called Pikeli, in Lithuania. It was so small we used to joke that you could stretch out your arms and touch both ends of town at once.

"You would have to cross all of America, the Atlantic Ocean,
and all of Europe to get there. How about we take a walk together,
and I'll tell you a story about me and Herschel in Pikeli."

"Now, this will be a long walk," Grandpa said. "I want to mail a package at the post office."

"Can I push the buttons on the stamp machine?" asked Walter.

"Sure you can," said Grandpa. "And you can carry the package. It's a birthday present for Herschel."

They started on their walk, and Grandpa started on his story.

"Back in Pikeli, everybody thought America was a wonderful
and strange place with gold in the streets, houses as beauti-
ful as palaces, and always enough to eat.
"But I wanted to come to America for another reason.

"I wanted to have the same freedom as everyone else, without anybody bothering me. I wanted to go to the same schools as everyone else, to live in the same places, to have the same jobs."

"But why couldn't you do those things, Grandpa?" Walter asked.

Grandpa sighed. "We weren't allowed. Because we were Jewish. We were bothered a lot, because people thought we were different."

"But everyone is different," said Walter. "Who wants to be all the same?"

"Smart question, Walter, but people aren't always so smart. Sometimes they're scared of what they don't understand. And when they're scared, they can be mean." Grandpa shook his head sadly.

"But in America," Grandpa went on, "everybody is different. Almost everybody comes from someplace else. Or if they don't, then their parents or grandparents did.

"Sure, people here can be mean, and there's certainly no gold in the streets. But it doesn't matter so much if I speak with an accent or have a big Jewish nose. So what?"

"Yeah," said Walter. "So what? And I like your big Jewish nose."

"Thank you," said Grandpa.

"Anyway," Grandpa continued, "I told Herschel that I was going to America, would he come with me? 'I can't,' he said. 'Why not?' I asked. 'In America we can live as we choose.' 'Maybe so,' said Herschel, 'but still I can't go.'

"'Why can't you?' I asked. 'I'm afraid,' said Herschel. 'It's too far. And maybe even what little we have here won't be there. I love prunes, and what if, in America, there are no prunes? I'll stay here with my prunes.' And he did."

"But Grandpa, there are prunes in America," said Walter. "Or you could eat raisins, apples, plums, bananas. Lots of fruit!"

"Yes," Grandpa said, nodding. "There are prunes here, but how could we know that then? As for bananas, we didn't even know what they were. The first time I saw one here, I ate the peel and

threw away the inside, because that's what you do with fruit—eat the outside and throw away the pit."

"You never saw a banana before?" Walter was astonished.

"Lots of things in America I'd never seen before." Grandpa smiled. "It was a new world for me."

"Anyway," Grandpa said, "it wasn't the prunes that kept Herschel home. He was afraid to leave what he knew for what he didn't know. And more than that, he treasured our old life, the songs and dances, the holidays, the family and friends."

"But Grandpa, weren't you scared to come to America all by yourself?" Walter asked. "Didn't you miss the old life?"

"Of course I missed it, and of course I was scared," Grandpa said. "There were prunes here, but in some ways Herschel was right. I lost forever those old, familiar ways of doing things. Still, it was more important to be free.

"It wasn't easy to come all that long way alone, but Herschel gave me a good-bye present. Prunes!"

"Prunes!" said Walter. "What a funny present!"

Grandpa smiled. "It was a good present. On that long, lonely journey, those prunes were a bit of Herschel, of the old life, with me. I made them last as long as I could, and I was sad when they were all gone. And you know what? Every year on my birthday, Herschel still sends me prunes."

"How old were you, Grandpa," Walter asked, "to go so far by yourself?"

"Well," said Grandpa, "still a boy, but older than you. I was ten."

They walked awhile without talking. Walter was thinking. Could he make the kind of journey Grandpa had? Or would he stay home like Herschel?

They came to a big, busy street. On the other side, Walter could see the American flag of the post office. Usually when he crossed a street, Walter held someone's hand, but he didn't want to do that now.

"Grandpa?"

"Yes?"

"I want to cross by myself. Let me. Please!"

Grandpa thought a minute. Then he smiled. "Well," he said, "you must be careful. When the light turns green, look both ways and make sure the cars have stopped. Wait for me at the curb. I'll be right behind you. Okay?"

Walter grinned. "Okay."

The light turned green. Walter looked both ways and made sure the cars had stopped. Then he turned and waved good-bye.

He felt very small and alone, but also excited. He gripped Herschel's package and started across the big, busy street.

When Walter got to the other side, he turned around with a smile. He felt big, very big.

"I did it, Grandpa!" he said. "I did it! Did you see?"

"I knew you could," Grandpa said.

"Grandpa?" asked Walter. "What's in this package, anyway? What do you send Herschel from America?"

"Prunes!" Grandpa laughed. "*American* prunes! That's what I send Herschel every year for his birthday."

Walter laughed too. "Grandpa? I'm glad you weren't afraid to come to America. I'm glad you came here so you could be my grandpa."

"Me too," said Grandpa. "Very glad."